P9-CSG-116

BINKY

THE SPACE CAT

KIDS CAN PRESS

For all the cats I've loved

Text and illustrations © 2009 Ashley Spires

All rights reserved. No part of this publication may be reproduced, stored in a retrieval system or transmitted, in any form or by any means, without the prior written permission of Kids Can Press Ltd. or, in case of photocopying or other reprographic copying, a license from The Canadian Copyright Licensing Agency (Access Copyright). For an Access Copyright license, visit www.accesscopyright.ca or call toll free to 1-800-893-5777.

Kids Can Press acknowledges the financial support of the Government of Ontario, through the Ontario Media Development Corporation's Ontario Book Initiative; the Ontario Arts Council; the Canada Council for the Arts; and the Government of Canada, through the BPIDP, for our publishing activity.

Published in Canada by
Kids Can Press Ltd.
25 Dockside Drive
Toronto, ON M5A 0B5

Published in the U.S. by
Kids Can Press Ltd.
2250 Military Road
Tonawanda, NY 14150

www.kidscanpress.com

The artwork in this book was rendered in ink, watercolor and cat fur.
The text is set in Fontoon.

Edited by Tara Walker
Designed by Karen Powers

The hardcover edition of this book is smyth sewn casebound.
The paperback edition of this book is limp sewn with a drawn-on cover.
Manufactured in Shen Zhen, Guang Dong, P.R. China, in 9/2010 by Printplus Limited

CM 09 0 9 8 7 6 5 4 3
CM PA 09 0 9 8 7 6 5

Library and Archives Canada Cataloguing in Publication

Spires, Ashley, 1978–
Binky the space cat / written and illustrated by Ashley Spires.

Interest age level: Ages 7 to 10.

ISBN 978-1-55453-309-1 (bound) ISBN 978-1-55453-419-7 (pbk.)

1. Cats—Juvenile fiction. I. Title. II. Series: Spires, Ashley, 1978– . Binky adventure.

PS8637.P57B55 2009 jC813'.6 C2009-900736-3

Kids Can Press is a Corus™ Entertainment company

Please note: No aliens, bugs or Space Cats were harmed in the making of this book. Okay, a mosquito was batted away a little too enthusiastically, and a fruit fly drowned under slightly suspicious circumstances, but that's all.
Space Cat's honor.

BINKY
THE SPACE CAT
by ASHLEY SPIRES
FTTTTTPT
PLOP
IT FINALLY CAME IN THE MAIL.
Yoink!

HE HAD BEEN WAITING FOR WEEKS.
squeak
click
SOMETHING THIS IMPORTANT REQUIRED COMPLETE PRIVACY.
TINK!
Riiiiiiiip!

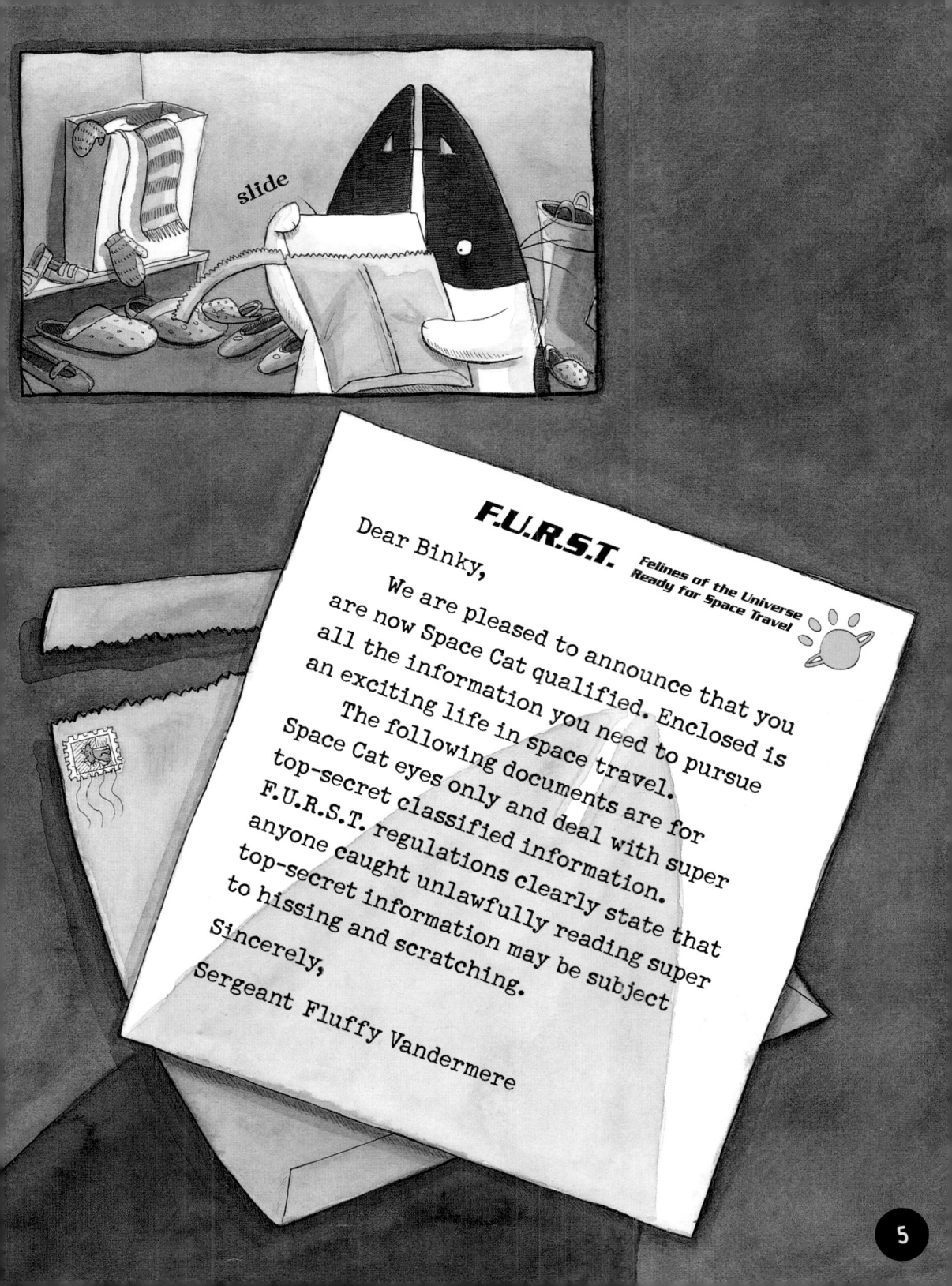
slide
F.U.R.S.T.
Felines of the Universe Ready for Space Travel
Dear Binky,
We are pleased to announce that you are now Space Cat qualified. Enclosed is all the information you need to pursue an exciting life in space travel.
The following documents are for Space Cat eyes only and deal with super top-secret classified information. F.U.R.S.T. regulations clearly state that anyone caught unlawfully reading super top-secret information may be subject to hissing and scratching.
Sincerely,
Sergeant Fluffy Vandermere

BINKY IS A SPACE CAT.
Space Cat Certified
NAME: Binky
COLOR: Black/White
FUR: Shorthair
BIRTH DATE: 12/07/06
89J43-PW
F.U.R.S.T.
Felines of the Universe Ready for Space Travel
OFFICIAL SPACE CAT BADGE

UNLIKE YOUR AVERAGE CAT ...
HE HAS A PURPOSE.

HIS MISSION IS TO ONE DAY BLAST OFF INTO OUTER SPACE ...
WHOOOSH!

TO EXPLORE UNKNOWN PLACES ...
bee-bop
bee-boppy
AND TO BATTLE ALIEN CREATURES.
MEOW!
HISS!
GRRR!
POW!

ACTUALLY, BINKY HASN'T EVER BEEN OUTSIDE.
TWEET
SWOOSH
sigh

HE LIVES HERE, IN THIS SPACE STATION, ENTIRELY SURROUNDED BY OUTER SPACE.
OUTER SPACE
DO NOT CROSS
DO NOT C
THAT'S WHY, UNTIL NOW, HE HAS HAD TO STAY INSIDE.
DANGER
DO NOT CROSS
ROSS
DO N
OUTER SPACE ISN'T SAFE FOR AN ORDINARY CAT.

IF BINKY WENT OUTSIDE WITHOUT PROPER PREPARATION, HE WOULDN'T BE ABLE TO BREATHE.
meow?
SNORT!
choke
(OUTER SPACE TENDS NOT TO HAVE OXYGEN.)

AND HE WOULD FLOAT AWAY.
meow?
MEOW!
meowwww

BINKY LIVES WITH ONE BIG HUMAN ...
ONE SMALL HUMAN ...
AND HIS MOUSIE, TED.
Prrrrrrrrrrrrrrrrrr
BINKY LOVES HIS HUMANS.
BOOK 1
HOW TO CARE FOR HUMANS
HE TAKES EXTREMELY GOOD CARE OF THEM.

HE GREETS THEM AT THE DOOR.

HE HELPS AROUND THE HOUSE.

HE GIVES THEM MASSAGES.

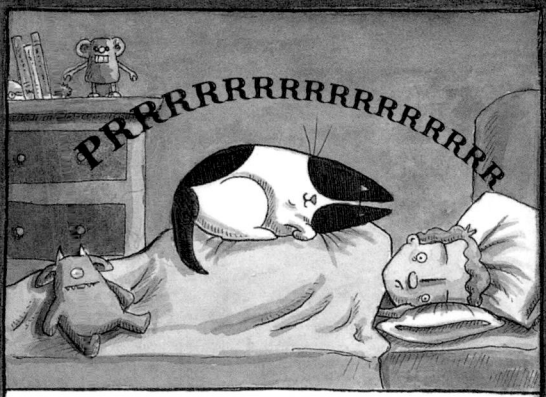

HE SINGS THEM TO SLEEP.

AND, MOST IMPORTANTLY, **HE PROTECTS THEM FROM ALIENS!!**

IN RETURN, BINKY'S HUMANS FEED HIM WELL ...
MAYBE TOO WELL ...
burp
prrrrrrrrr
AND GIVE HIM CUDDLES.

HE MAKES A MENTAL NOTE TO SEND THEM A POSTCARD FROM OUTER SPACE.
dear humans,
i am in
outer space.
i miss you both.
watch out
for aliens.
love Binky
big and small humans
42 Sentinel Parkway,
Spuzzum

WHEN BINKY FIRST ARRIVED AT 42 SENTINEL PARKWAY, HE WAS JUST A KITTEN.
Come on out, Binky!
Come meet your new mousie!
mew?
meow!
prrrrrrrrrrrrrrrrrrrr

bzzzzzzzz
DESPITE HIS YOUNG AGE, HE QUICKLY REALIZED ...
bzzzzz
THAT ALIENS ...
WERE ...
bzzzzzz
bzzzzzzz
EVERYWHERE!!

bzzz

BINKY TRIED TO FLY ONCE.
whoosh!
meoooooooowww!
SPLAT!
IT HURT.

BINKY ALSO NOTICED THAT HIS HUMANS KEPT REFERRING TO THE ALIENS AS "BUGS."
A bug!
Ew, bugs!
Na nug!
Another bug!

?
bzzzzzzzzzzzz
LIKE ANY CURIOUS KITTEN ...
BINKY DECIDED TO DO SOME RESEARCH.
zzzzzzzzzzzzzzzzzzz

ALIEN QUALITIES	BUG QUALITIES
- can fly - have big eyes - steal your food - lay eggs - technologically advanced species who have mastered space travel	- can fly - have big eyes - steal your food - lay eggs - eat poo

BINKY DREW THREE CONCLUSIONS:

1. OBVIOUSLY, BUGS AND ALIENS ARE THE SAME THING.

2. TOO BAD HUMANS AREN'T SMART ENOUGH TO FIGURE THIS OUT.

3. THAT MUST BE WHY THEY NEED A CAT AROUND.

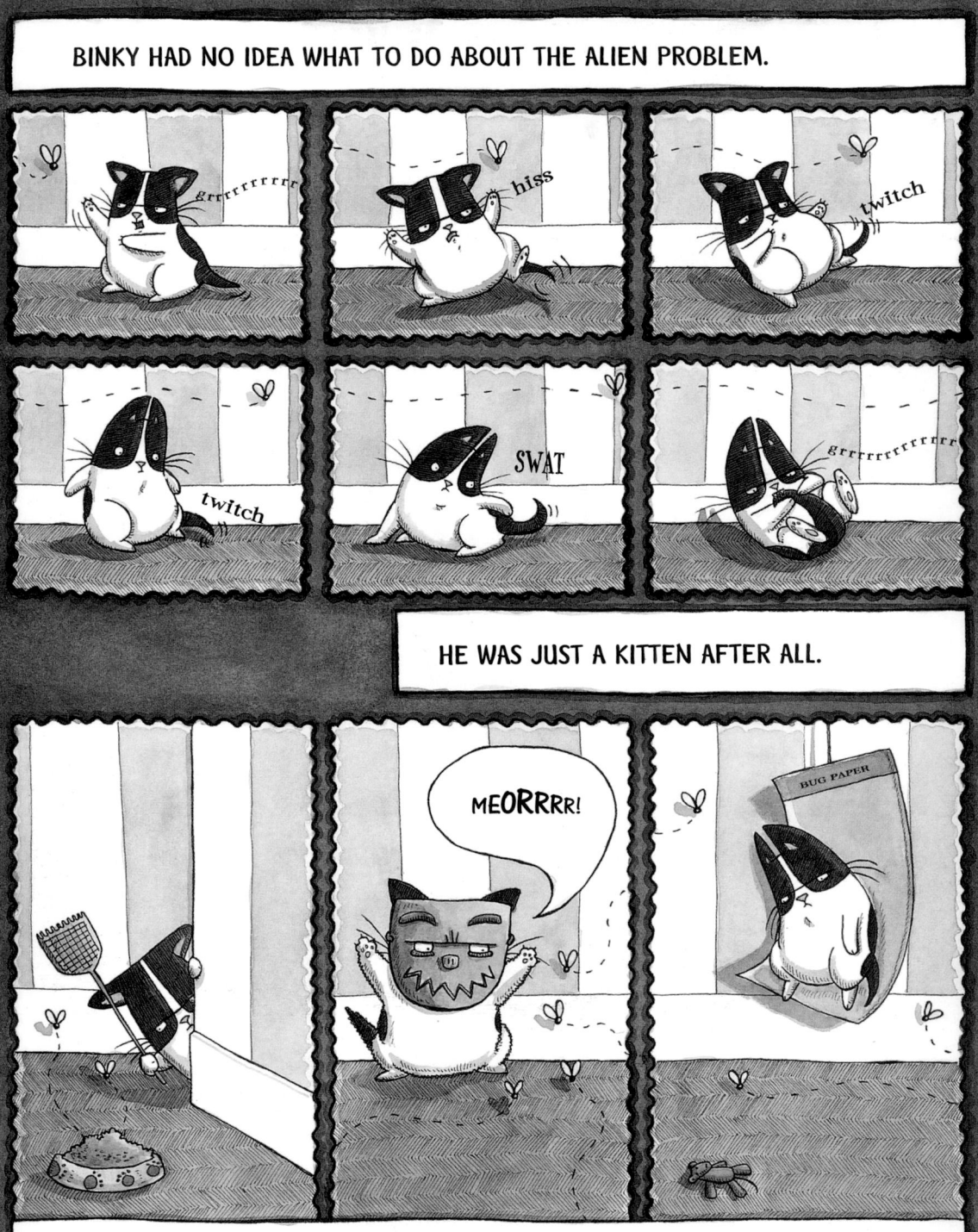
BINKY HAD NO IDEA WHAT TO DO ABOUT THE ALIEN PROBLEM.
grrrrrrrrrr
hiss
twitch
twitch
SWAT
grrrrrrrrrrrr
HE WAS JUST A KITTEN AFTER ALL.
MEORRRR!
BUG PAPER
HE TRIED A FEW THINGS, BUT NOTHING WORKED.

THEN ONE DAY, HE FOUND SOMETHING AT THE BOTTOM OF HIS KITTY FOOD BAG.
rustle
rustle
munch
munch
F.U.R.S.T.
Want to stop aliens? Then become a SPACE CAT today!!!
FROM THAT MOMENT ON, BINKY WAS DETERMINED TO BE A SPACE CAT.

BINKY'S HUMANS HAVE NO IDEA THAT HE IS NOW A REAL SPACE CAT ...
Space Cat Manual
SLAM!
Who's the cutest kitty?
PROTECTING THEM FROM ALIEN DOMINATION.
zooom
(AS MENTIONED EARLIER, THEY AREN'T VERY BRIGHT.)

IT'S IMPERATIVE THAT HIS IDENTITY REMAIN A SECRET.
gasp!
IF ONE OF THE ALIEN SPIES WERE TO FIND OUT ...
bzzz bzzz bzzz Space Cat bzzz bzzz
WHO HE REALLY IS ...
bzzzz bzzzzzzzzz bzzzzzzz bzzzzz
MEOW!!!
THE ALIENS COULD MOUNT AN ATTACK ...
bzzzzzzzzz
THAT EVEN BINKY, AN OFFICIAL CERTIFIED SPACE CAT, COULDN'T DEFEAT.
PUNT!

AND THEN WHAT?
HE AND HIS HUMANS WOULD BE ENSLAVED BY THE FLYING MENACES AND FORCED TO DO HORRIBLE THINGS ...
GAG!
Ewwww!
BLECH!
LIKE EAT VEGETABLES ...
VRRRRRRRRR
OR STAY IN THE SAME ROOM AS THE VACUUM ...

bzzzzzz
bzzzzzzz
OR LEAVE THE KITTY LITTER BOX UNSCOOPED!
IT'S ALMOST TOO TERRIBLE TO IMAGINE!

IN ORDER TO PREVENT THIS KIND OF ALIEN INVASION ...
BINKY PATROLS THE PERIMETER.
HE ELIMINATES THE ALIENS WHO ARE DARING ENOUGH ...
bzzzzzzzzzzzzzz
TO SNEAK INTO HIS SPACE STATION.
GULP!

ONE OF THE BASIC RULES OF BEING A SPACE CAT IS TO CONSTANTLY TRAIN AGAINST ALIEN ATTACKS.
PRETEND ALIEN
KAPOW!
BINKY TRAINS VERY HARD.

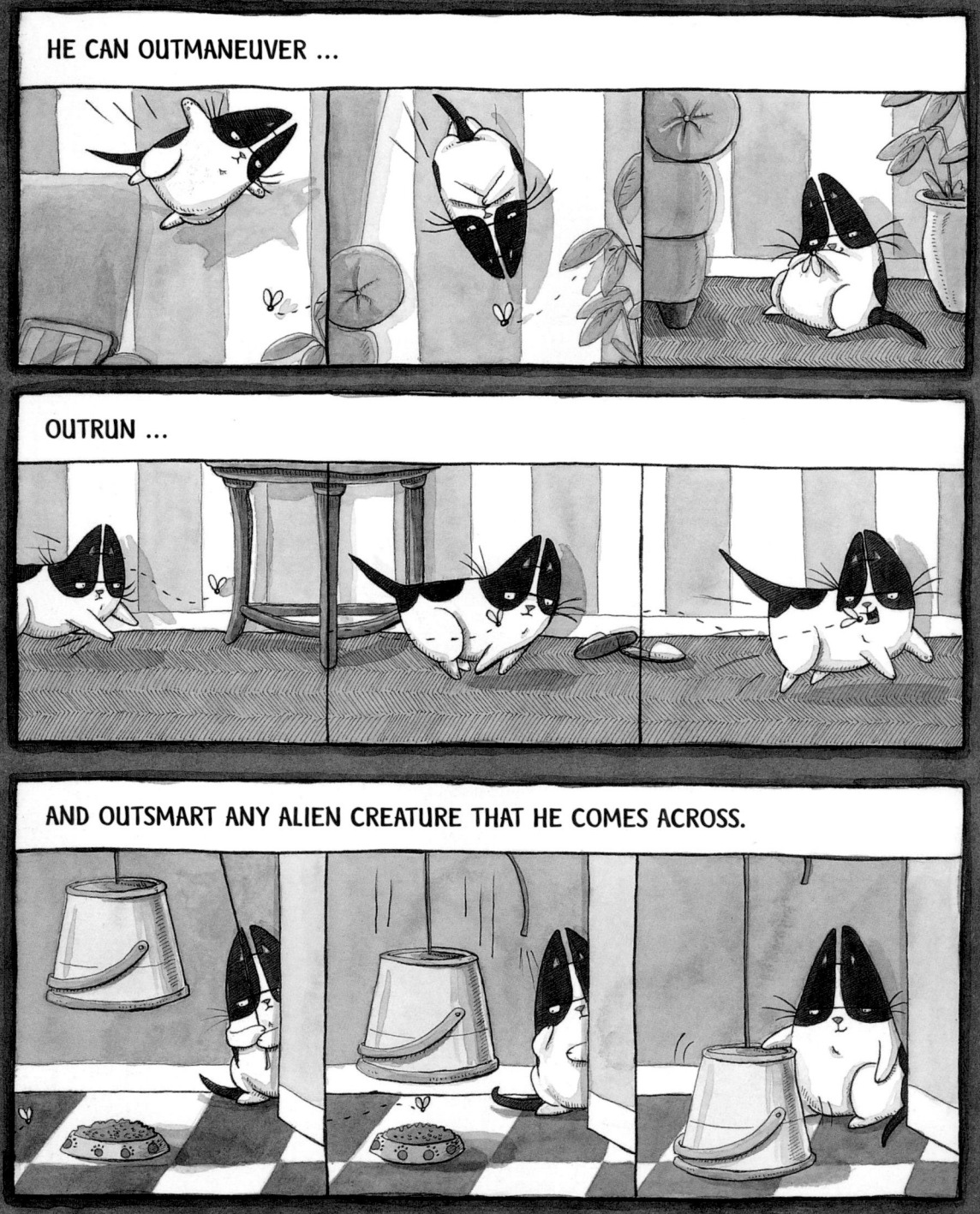
HE CAN OUTMANEUVER ...
OUTRUN ...
AND OUTSMART ANY ALIEN CREATURE THAT HE COMES ACROSS.

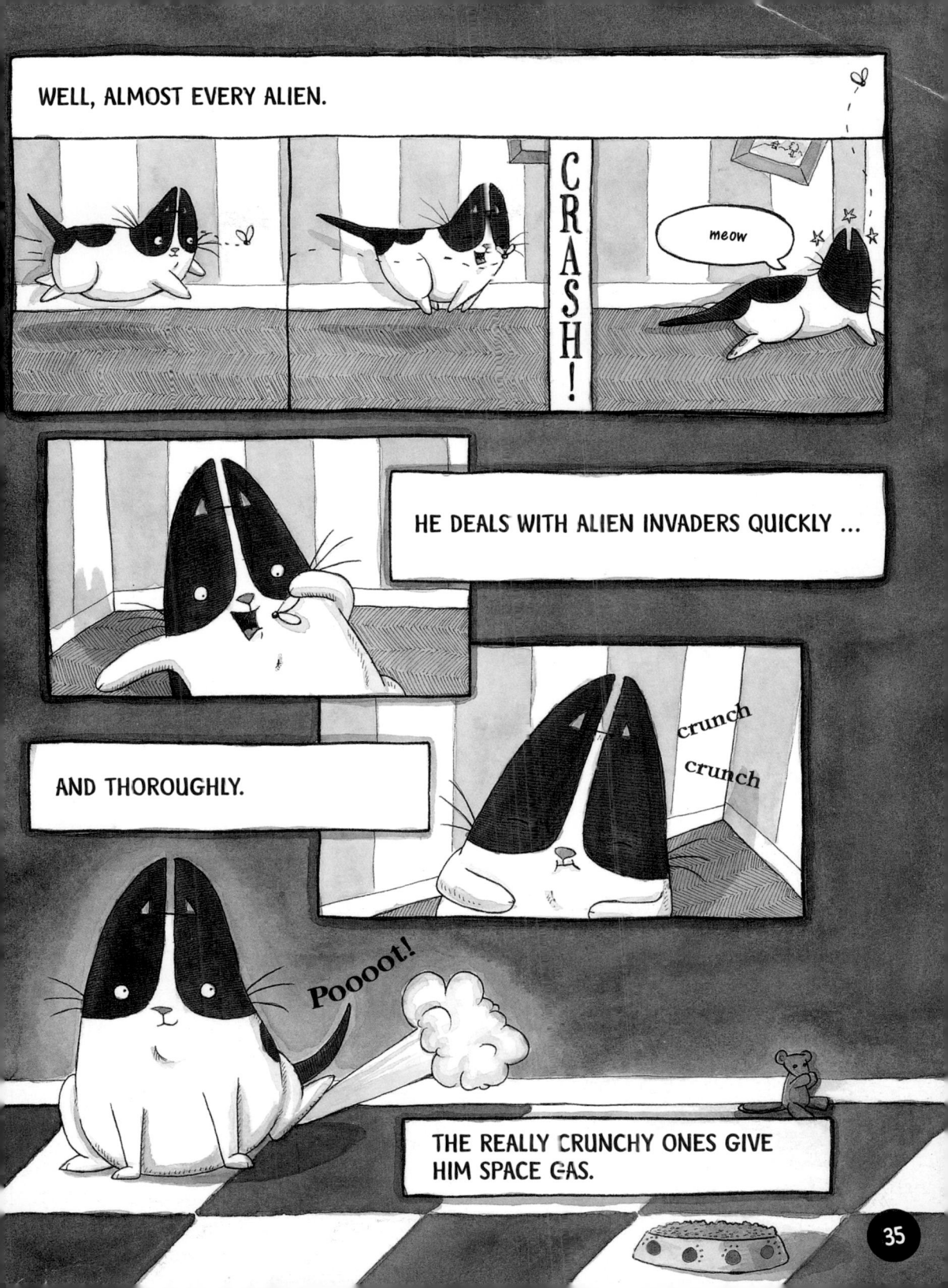
WELL, ALMOST EVERY ALIEN.
CRASH!
meow
HE DEALS WITH ALIEN INVADERS QUICKLY ...
crunch
crunch
AND THOROUGHLY.
Poooot!
THE REALLY CRUNCHY ONES GIVE HIM SPACE GAS.

ZOOOOOM!
BINKY KNOWS THAT IN ORDER TO SPACE TRAVEL, YOU NEED A ROCKET SHIP ...
SPACE SHIPS!
One small step ...
OR, AT THE VERY LEAST, AN AIRTIGHT ASTRONAUT SUIT.

HE HAS SEEN HIS HUMANS PUT ON THEIR SPECIAL SPACE SUITS WHENEVER THEY GO OUT.
snap
squish
slip
flup
shloooop
ziiip
Bye, Binky! See you soon.
Love you, Binky!

BINKY WORRIES ABOUT HIS HUMANS ...
OUT THERE ALL ALONE ...
AAAAAAAAAAAA!
MEOW!
WITH NO SPACE CAT TO PROTECT THEM.

ONE DAY HE TRIED ON SOME OF THEIR SPACE GEAR, HOPING HE COULD GO WITH THEM.
trip
MEOW!
bump
CRASH!
IT DIDN'T WORK.

SINCE HE DOESN'T HAVE A SPACE SUIT ...
lick
lick
BINKY HAS NO CHOICE ...
ZIIIP!
BUT TO BUILD HIS OWN ROCKET SHIP!

ROCKET SHIP
PLANS
SPACE CAT
Introductory
Package
FORTUNATELY, DETAILED ROCKET SHIP BLUEPRINTS ARE INCLUDED WITH EVERY SPACE CAT INTRODUCTORY PACKAGE.
F.U.R.S.T.
You're a Space Cat, Now What?
CHAPTER 3: How to Build a Rocket Ship with Things You Can Steal from Your Humans

DURING THE DAY ...
OR DURING THE NIGHT ...
poot!
WHENEVER BINKY CAN SLIP AWAY UNNOTICED ...
TOP SECRET
No Humans AND DEFINITELY NO ALIENS!
HE GETS TO WORK BUILDING HIS ROCKET SHIP.

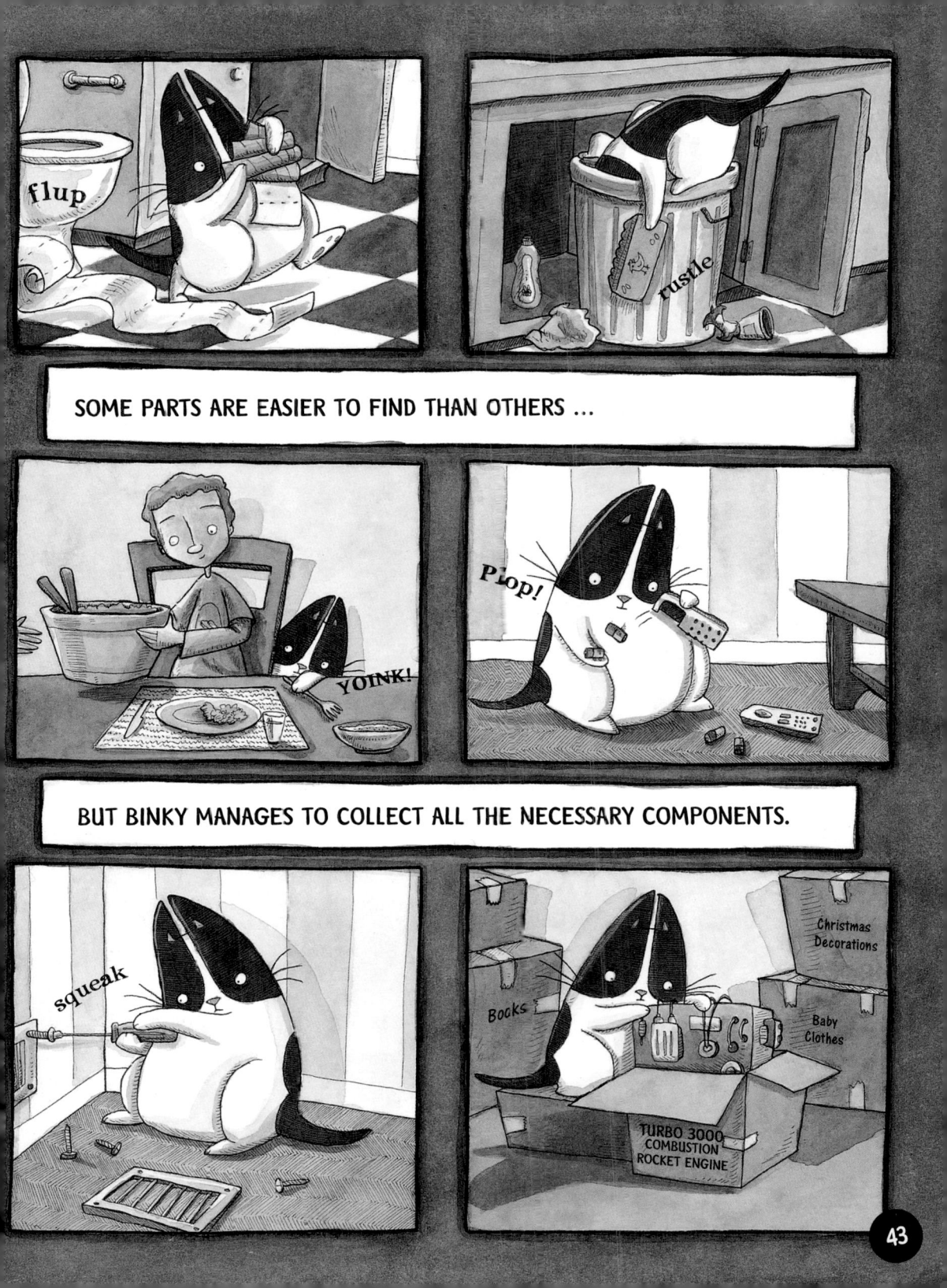
flup
rustle
SOME PARTS ARE EASIER TO FIND THAN OTHERS ...
YOINK!
Plop!
BUT BINKY MANAGES TO COLLECT ALL THE NECESSARY COMPONENTS.
squeak
Christmas Decorations
Books
Baby Clothes
TURBO 3000 COMBUSTION ROCKET ENGINE

PZZZZZZZZZZZZZZZ!
TUCKED AWAY IN HIS LITTER BOX ...
wusha wusha
BINKY PREPARES FOR HIS MISSION.
CLONK!
HIS SHIP IS COMING TOGETHER NICELY.

ZZZZZZ
BUT HE HAS TO BE CAREFUL.
SECRET ROCKET SHIP BLUEPRINTS
click!
SWIPE!
YIPES!
crunch
crunch
THE ENEMY IS ALWAYS WATCHING.

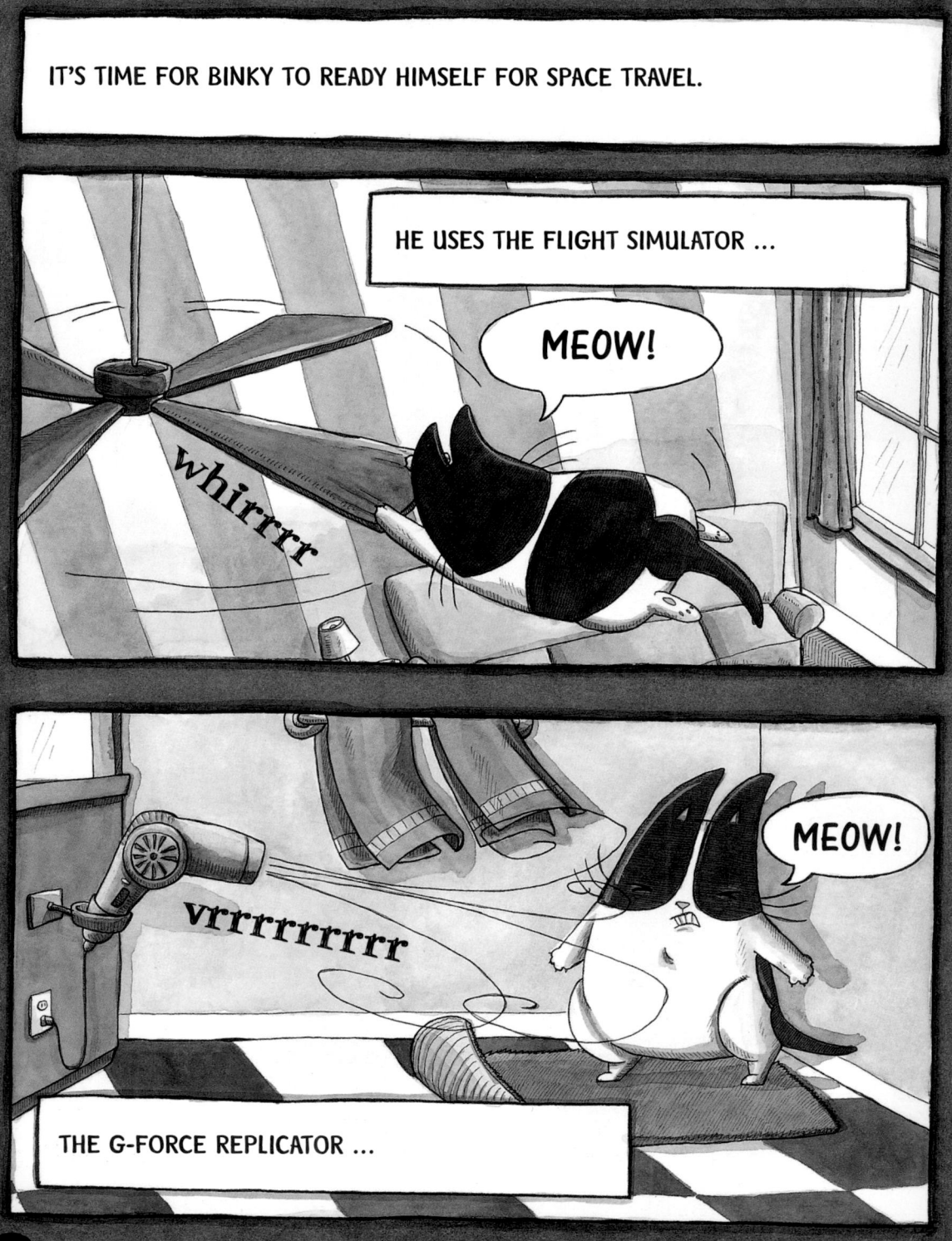
IT'S TIME FOR BINKY TO READY HIMSELF FOR SPACE TRAVEL.
HE USES THE FLIGHT SIMULATOR ...
MEOW!
whirrrr
MEOW!
vrrrrrrrrr
THE G-FORCE REPLICATOR ...

DISCLAIMER: BINKY IS A TRAINED SPACE CAT. CATS AND HUMANS SHOULD NEVER GO IN THE DRYER. EVER.

SPACE TRAVEL TRAINING IS NOT EASY.

IT FREQUENTLY LEADS TO HAIR BALLS.

AND SO BINKY TRAINS ...

AND BUILDS ...

AND FIGHTS ...

AND CUDDLES ...

AND TRAINS ...

AND BUILDS ...

lick
AND WASHES ...
hissssssss
AND FIGHTS ...
tink
tink
AND BUILDS ...
zzzzzzzzzzzzz
AND NAPS ...
pooot!
AND TRAINS ...
GASP
UNTIL FINALLY ONE DAY ...

HIS ROCKET SHIP IS COMPLETE!

rattle
WITH A LITTLE ROCKET FUEL ...
rattle
SOME SPACE SNACKS ...
splish!
HIS SPACE HELMET ...
AND HIS TRUSTY COPILOT ...
BINKY IS FINALLY READY FOR OUTER SPACE!

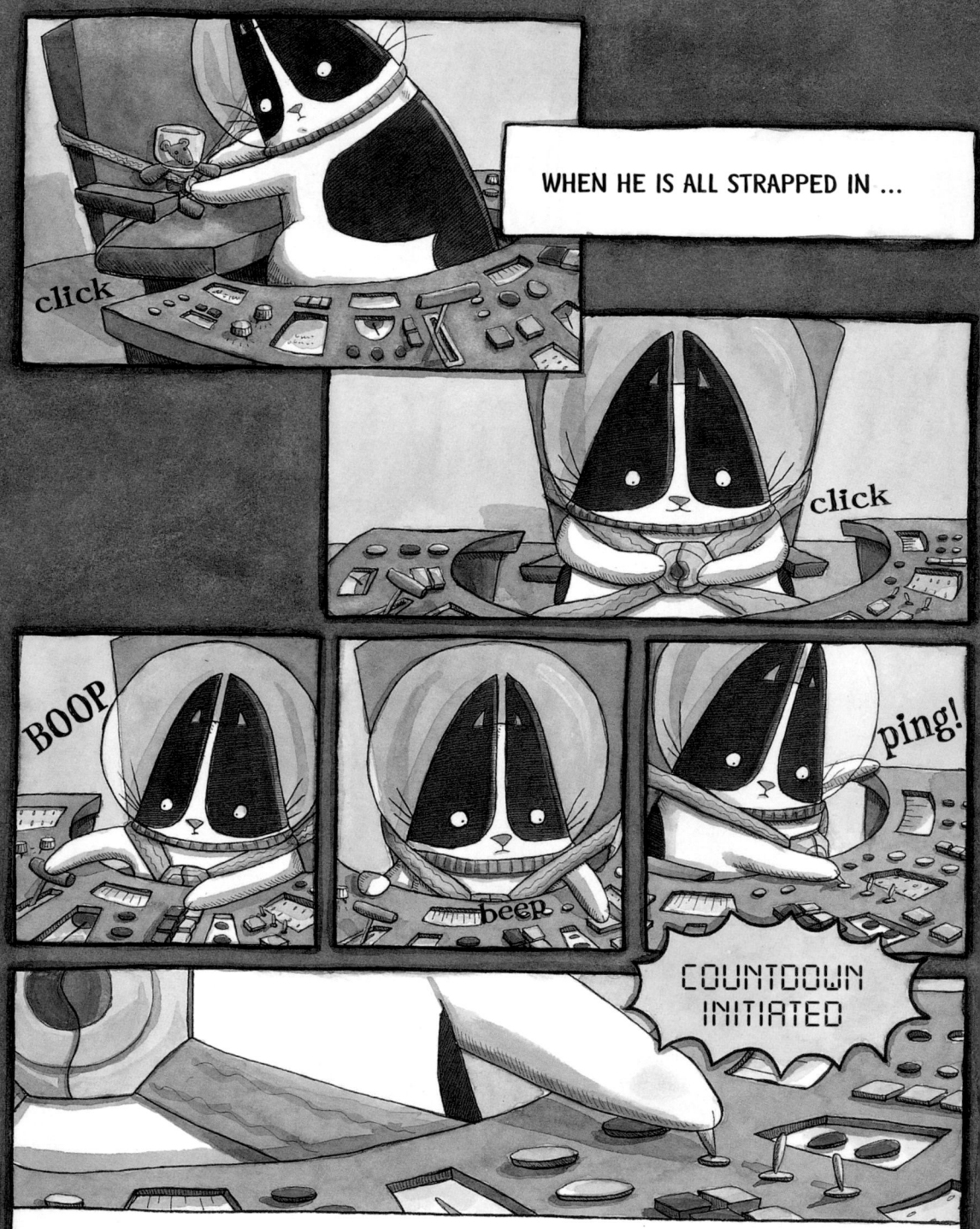

BINKY THE SPACE CAT STARTS THE COUNTDOWN TO BLASTOFF.

5
HE IS ALL PACKED AND READY TO GO ON THE ADVENTURE OF A LIFETIME.
YET BINKY FEELS LIKE SOMETHING IS MISSING ...

4

HE'S SURE HE HAS PACKED EVERYTHING.

F.U.R.S.T.

- ☑ space helmet
- ☑ snacks
- ☑ copilot
- ☑ planet guide
- ☑ alien fighting gloves
- ☑ zero-gravity kitty litter

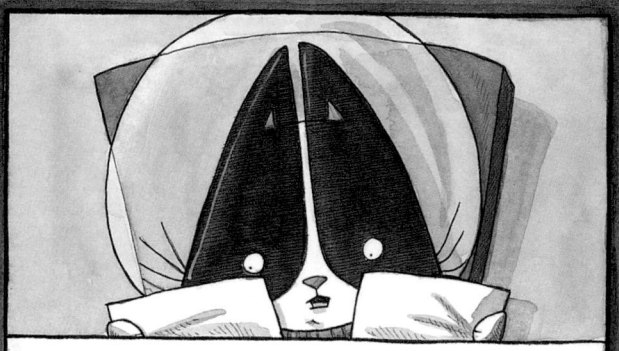

BUT THEN HE REALIZES ...

SOMETHING VERY IMPORTANT IS **NOT** ON HIS LIST.

THE MOST IMPORTANT THING OF ALL ...

3

GASP!
HIS HUMANS!!!

2
zoooom!
IF HE LEAVES WITHOUT THEM ...
Binky! Help us!
THEN WHO WILL PROTECT HIS HUMANS FROM ALIEN INVADERS?

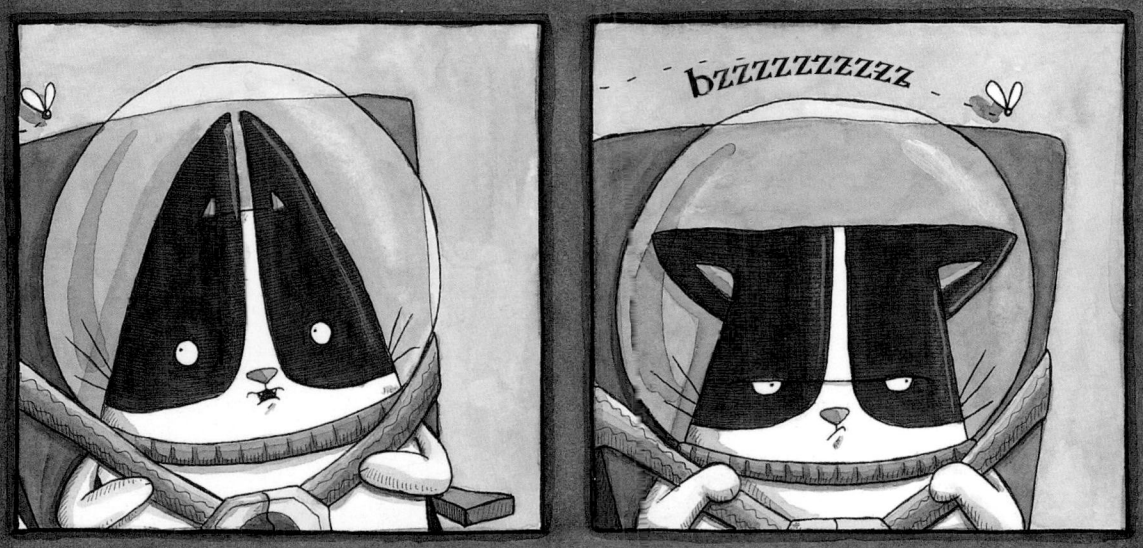

WHAT KIND OF A SPACE CAT WOULD HE BE IF HE LEFT THEM BEHIND?

BINKY KNOWS THERE IS ONLY ONE THING TO DO ...

1
BCCCCHHHHH.

RUMBLE
RUMBLE
whooosh!

ALL OF BINKY'S DREAMS OF OUTER SPACE ADVENTURE HAVE DISAPPEARED OUT THE WINDOW.
WHOOOSH!

CRASH!
NO MORE EXPLORING NEW WORLDS.
POP!
NO MORE ALIEN SPACE CHASES.
toss
NO MORE BINKY, SPACE CAT EXTRAORDINAIRE.
BINKY!

bzzzzzzzz
HELP!!
bzzzzzzzzzzzzz
AAAAAAAAAAAA
GULP!

scratch
crunch
Thank goodness you were here, Binky!
CLEARLY, BINKY MADE THE RIGHT CHOICE.
Come here, Brave Kitty!
HIS HUMANS ARE UTTERLY HELPLESS WITHOUT HIM.
PLUS, WHO WOULD GIVE HIM CUDDLES WAY OUT IN OUTER SPACE?
PRRRRRRRRRRRRRRRRRRRRRR

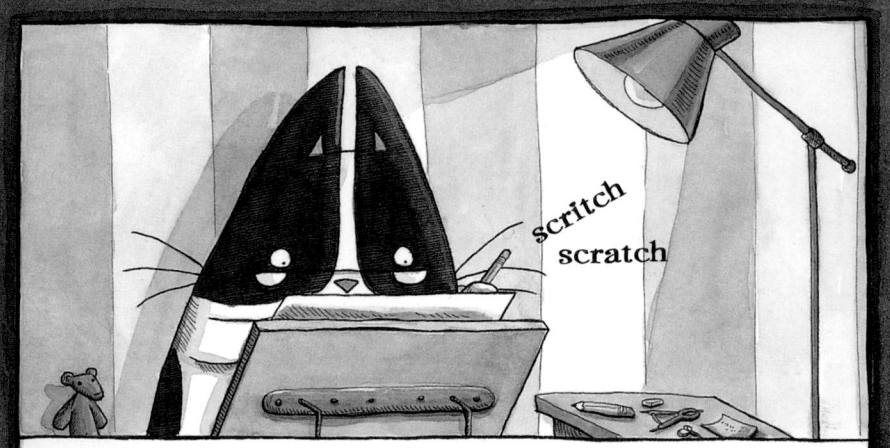

BINKY HAS LEARNED SOMETHING VERY IMPORTANT ...

NEXT TIME, BUILD A BIGGER ROCKET SHIP.